HENRY

JAMES

PERCY

TITLES AVAILABLE IN BUZZ BOOKS

First published 1990 by Buzz Books,
an imprint of the Octopus Publishing Group,
Michelin House, 81 Fulham Road, London SW3 6RB

LONDON MELBOURNE AUCKLAND

Copyright © William Heinemann Ltd 1990

ISBN 1 85591 005 5

Printed and bound in the UK

THOMAS
GOES FISHING

buzz books

Thomas the Tank Engine had his own branch line. It was his reward for helping James, the Red Engine. The trucks had pushed James off the rails and Thomas had helped to rescue him.

Thomas was very proud of his branch line. Every day he puffed up and down with his two coaches, Annie and Clarabel. He always looked forward to something special . . . the river.

As he rumbled over the bridge he would
see people fishing down below. He often
wanted to stay and watch.

But his driver always said, "No! What
would the Fat Controller say if we were
late?"

Thomas still thought it would be lovely to stop by the river and do some fishing.

Every time Thomas met another engine, he would say, "I want to fish."

But they all gave the same answer, "Engines don't go fishing!"

And that's just what James said as he passed Thomas that day.

10

One day, Thomas stopped as usual to take in water at the station by the river. Then he saw a big painted notice. It read, "OUT OF ORDER".

OUT OF
ORDER

Thomas was very thirsty. The driver had
an idea. They could get water from the
river!

They found a bucket and some rope and
went to the bridge. Then the driver let the
bucket down into the water.

The bucket was old and had five holes.

So they had to fill it, pull it up, and empty it into Thomas's tank as quickly as they could, again and again.

At last they were finished.

"That's good! That's good!" puffed Thomas, as he started off again, with Annie and Clarabel running happily behind.

They puffed along the valley until suddenly, Thomas began to feel a pain in his boiler. Steam began to hiss from his safety valve in an alarming way.

"There's too much steam," said his driver.

The fireman tried to let more water into the boiler, but none came.

"Oh dear!" groaned Thomas. "I'm going to burst! I'm going to burst!"

They damped down his fire and he struggled on.

"I've got such a pain! I've got such a pain!" Thomas hissed.

They stopped outside the last station and Annie and Clarabel were uncoupled. The driver ran Thomas onto a siding, right out of the way.

DANGER
KEEP

He was still hissing, fit to burst.
Then the guard telephoned for an Engine
Inspector and the driver found two notices.
They were written in large letters and read,
"DANGER. KEEP AWAY".

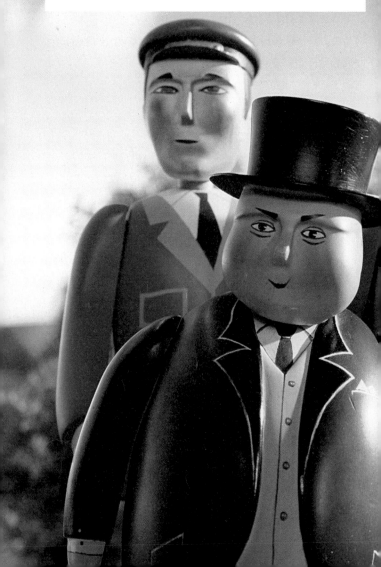

Soon the Inspector and the Fat Controller arrived.

"Cheer up, Thomas!" they said. "We'll soon put you right."

The driver told them what had happened.
The Engine Inspector thought that the
trouble must be in the feed pipe.

The Inspector climbed up to have a look. He peered in and then came down.

"Excuse me, sir," he said. "Please look in the tank and tell me what you see."

So the Fat Controller clambered up, looked in and nearly fell off in surprise!

DANGER
KEEP
AWAY

"Inspector," he whispered, "can you see *fish*?"

"Gracious, goodness me! How did the fish get there, Driver?" asked the Inspector.

"We must have fished them out of the river with our bucket!" said Thomas's driver.

"Well, Thomas. So you and your driver have been fishing. But fish don't suit you. We must get them out," said the Fat Controller.

They took turns at fishing in Thomas's tank. The Fat Controller looked on and told them how to do it.

DANGER
KEEP
AWAY

· When they had caught all the fish, they had a lovely picnic supper of fish and chips.

"That was good!" said the Fat Controller, as he finished off his share. "But fish don't suit *you*, Thomas. So you mustn't do it again."

"No, sir, I won't," said Thomas sadly. "Engines don't go fishing. It's too uncomfortable!"

THOMAS

EDWARD

GORDON